Holding On To
The Memories

By: Britt Wolfe

Copyright © 2025 Britt Wolfe

All rights reserved. No part of this book may be reproduced, distributed, or transmitted in any form or by any means, including (but not limited to) photocopying, recording, or telepathic osmosis, without prior written permission from the author.

This is a work of fiction. Any resemblance to actual persons, living or dead, is purely coincidental—unless you feel personally attacked, in which case, maybe do some self-reflection. The characters and events in this book are entirely products of the author's imagination, and any similarities to real life are either accidental or a sign that the simulation is glitching.

Cover design, formatting, and caffeine consumption by Britt Wolfe. Additional emotional support provided by Sophie and Lena.

First Edition: 2025

Printed in Canada because books deserve a solid passport stamp too.

For inquiries, praise, declarations of undying love, or to request permission for use beyond fair dealing (seriously, just ask first), please visit: BrittWolfe.com

If you enjoyed this book, please consider leaving a review. If you didn't, well, that's between you and your questionable taste.

This Novella Is Dedicated to:

The women who become lifelines.

To the friendships that don't just withstand the storms—they anchor us through them.

To the ladies who show up without being asked, who hear the unspoken words beneath the silence, and who know exactly when to make us laugh and when to simply sit beside us.

You are the ones who have made every season of life brighter, every heartache softer, and every triumph sweeter. Across miles and years, through belly laughs and broken moments, we've built something unbreakable.

You are my chosen sisters, my forever people—the kind of friends most only dream of finding. My life is endlessly richer because of you. This story is, and always will be, yours.

Holding On To The Memories
Is Inspired by: *New Year's Day*
by Taylor Swift

New Year's Day was my immediate favourite from *Reputation*. The moment I heard it, I listened to it over and over, unable to get enough of its gentle, heartfelt melody and poignant lyrics. Since the album's release, it's been the song that wakes me up every morning, the first sound I hear to start my day.

To me, though I don't think Taylor intended it is this way, New Year's Day has always been more than just a love song—it's a song about female friendship. Every time I hear it, I think of the incredible women I am lucky enough to have in my life, the ones who have stood beside me through everything, and who I have had the immense privilege to stand beside through their own triumphs, trials and tribulations. This song reminds me of how important these friendships are, how our paths crossed in ways that feel almost magical, and how our bond has endured for 20, 30, even 40 years.

I never want to forget their laughter, the small moments and memories that have woven our lives together. I will always be there for them, just as they have always been there for me. And I definitely look forward to celebrating many more New Year's Days with them, holding on to the memories and creating new ones, year after year.

This story, inspired by Taylor Swift's extraordinary words, is my tribute to the beauty and resilience of female friendship—to the love that stays, the memories that linger, and the unwavering support that carries us through every season of life.

Peace, Love, and Inspiration,

Britt Wolfe

The Letter
New Years ~ Present Day

The house was steeped in the kind of warmth that only years of love and laughter could create. The soft glow of string lights shimmered against the windows, casting delicate patterns onto the hardwood floor. The scent of cinnamon and evergreen lingered in the air, weaving through the faint echoes of laughter. Ben, Liam, and little Chester were sprawled across the couch in their mismatched pyjamas, their faces sticky from too many desserts, their eyelids heavy but determined to fight sleep—stretching out the magic of the holiday just a little longer.

At the kitchen sink, Maddy stood with her hands submerged in warm, soapy water, gazing out at the snow drifting in soft, silent sheets against the dark Pennsylvania sky. The twinkling lights from the neighbours' houses glowed faintly in the distance, but she barely noticed. Her heart felt suspended somewhere between the past and the present, between the undeniable beauty of this evening and the bittersweet weight of New Year's Eves gone by.

This is her favourite night of the year. Was the thought caught in Maddy's mind.

Or at least, it had been.

Before.

The quiet padding of bare feet down the hallway caught Maddy's attention. She turned to see Derrick standing in the doorway between the hallway and their open-plan kitchen and living room, his broad shoulders framed by the soft glow of the hall lights. His face was etched with something warm yet weighted—tender but heavy, as if he were carrying more than just his thoughts. In his hand, he held an envelope, its edges slightly worn, the paper softened by time, as though it had been carried close for far too long.

"Mads," he said quietly, his voice barely rising above the soft hum of the house at this late hour of the night. "I've got something for you."

She frowned, wiping her hands on the dish towel slung over her shoulder. "What is it?" she asked.

Derrick stepped closer, his eyes never leaving hers. "It's from Eve."

For a moment, the world seemed to slip sideways, tilting beneath Maddy like a violent earthquake. The warmth of the house, the laughter, the golden flicker of the fireplace—it all dulled, shrinking to the edges of her awareness as a wave of something heavy and unnameable settled deep in her chest. Maddy's fingers pressed against the cool quartz of the countertop, the contrast shocking against the heat rushing through her veins, her heart pounding in a frantic, uneven rhythm. The boys' tired giggles became a muffled echo, the steady tick of the clock blurred into nothing, lost beneath the sound of her own pulse crashing in her ears. The moment stretched, bending around her, holding her in place while everything else slipped just out of reach.

Maddy stared at the envelope in Derrick's hand. She recognized Eve's handwriting instantly—the familiar, looping letters that had filled birthday cards, grocery lists stuck to Eve's fridge, and notes passed in class when they were kids. Maddy's breath caught in her throat, and she reached out, her fingers trembling as they closed around the paper.

"She asked me to give it to you tonight," Derrick said softly, his voice low and thick with emotion. He glanced down at the envelope in his hand, his grip tightening even as Maddy reached for it. He held onto it, not out of reluctance, but because he needed her to understand—really understand—why he had waited. Why he had kept this piece of Eve from her for so long. His gaze flickered to hers, searching, as if trying to find the words before finally releasing the envelope into her trembling grasp. "At midnight."

Maddy's breath caught, her gaze fixed on the familiar handwriting. But Derrick didn't let go of the envelope just yet.

"I'll be honest," he continued, his voice trembling slightly. "It felt wrong… keeping this from you. I've had it for so long, and every part of me wanted to give it to you sooner, especially after she passed." He let out a slow breath, his thumb brushing over the edge of the envelope like he was still trying to make sense of it all. "But Eve—she knew what she was doing."

He finally met Maddy's eyes, his voice growing steadier as he spoke, as if saying the words out loud helped him believe them. "We talked about it, right near the end. The last time I saw her. When she realized she wasn't going to make it to the New Year.

"She said New Year's was always your guys' night. Your favourite holiday, your time together. She wanted you to have this when the year was fresh and full of promise, not in the middle of all that pain. She wanted this letter to be a beginning, not an ending."

Derrick's hand lingered on the envelope for just a moment longer, his touch a silent reassurance, in the tumultuous emotions roaring through Maddy. "And now, standing here, I get it. I know why she asked me to wait."

His voice softened, and when he finally released the envelope into Maddy's trembling hands, his eyes were full of the same love and respect that had carried them all through this loss. "She wanted you to start this year with her, not just with the memory of losing her."

Maddy swallowed hard, feeling the weight of the letter settle into her chest before she even opened it. She nodded, though her voice was lost somewhere in the knot of her throat, and Derrick stepped back, giving her the space to face this one last gift from Eve—the one that would carry her into the new year, and maybe, just maybe, help her find a way forward.

She nodded for Derrick to take the boys to bed before she slipped out the back door, into the crisp night air. The cold bit at her skin, sharp and immediate, but she welcomed it. It was comforting in its relentlessness. Real. She made her way to the old wooden swing on the porch—the same one where she and Eve had sat countless times before, wrapped in blankets, whispering about everything and nothing as the new year crept in around them.

The sky above was a blanket of stars, the snow falling in soft, silent flakes, each one catching the light like tiny, fleeting miracles.

With a shaky breath, Maddy opened the envelope.

The letter inside was folded neatly, the paper soft and worn from Eve's touch. Maddy unfolded it with care, as if the weight of her grief might tear it apart. After a deep breath, she began to read.

Maddy,

I don't know how to start this letter because it feels impossible to find the right words when I know I'm leaving you behind. I guess I just want you to know that I've thought about this moment more times than I can count. I thought about what I'd say, how I'd say it, and nothing ever felt like enough.

And maybe that's the point. Maybe there are no perfect words for this kind of thing. For endings. But if I've learned anything in all the years I've been lucky enough to call you my best friend, it's that showing up matters more than saying the right thing. So here I am, showing up for you the only way I still can.

You were my first friend, Maddy. The first person who ever saw me, really saw me, and didn't let go. Do you remember that day on the bus? I was so scared, so sure I'd never belong anywhere, and then there you were–this bold, fearless little girl with messy red curls and a gap-toothed smile, reaching for my hand like it was the most natural thing in the world. You held on tight, and you never let go.

You have no idea how much that meant to me. How much it still means.

You've held my hand through everything. The good, the bad, the beautiful, the heartbreakingly hard, and through an ending. You were there when my mom got sick, when Sebastian and I couldn't have the family we dreamed of, when the world felt like it was crumbling beneath my feet. You were there when I was scared to admit I was tired of fighting, when I couldn't find the strength to say out loud what we both knew was coming. You never asked me to be anything other than exactly who I was–broken pieces and all.

And that's what I want for you now.

I want you to know that it's okay to be sad. It's okay to miss me. I hope you do miss me. But I also hope you keep living the beautiful, messy, wonderful life you've built. I hope you keep laughing with Derrick and dancing in the kitchen with the boys. I hope you keep running Once Upon A Latte and filling it with stories and light and warmth. I hope you keep making new memories, even when it feels like you shouldn't.

Because you deserve that, Maddy. You deserve all the joy and love this world has to offer. And I want you to grab hold of it with both hands.

I know you're probably sitting there right now, reading this, and wondering how you're supposed to do this without me. And the truth is, I don't have the answer. I wish I did. God, if we're wishing, I wish I didn't have to write this letter at all. I wish we had another year, another decade, another lifetime. But if there's one thing I do know, it's that you will keep going—because that's who you are. You don't just survive, Maddy. You love, you carry, you hold the people around you together even when you feel like you're breaking. And even in the moments when it feels impossible, when the weight of this loss is too much to bear, I know—I know—you'll find a way to keep moving forward. Not because you have to. But because you have so much left to live for.

Because that's who you are.

You are the bravest, kindest, most stubborn person I've ever known. You've carried me through more than I can put into words, and now it's time to carry yourself. But you don't have to do it alone. You have Derrick, who loves you more than life itself, and those beautiful boys who will grow up knowing that their mom is a force of nature. And you have me.

I'm still here, Maddy.

I'm in the quiet mornings when the world is just waking up. I'm in the first snowfall of the year, in the smell of fresh coffee and old books, in the sound of your boys' laughter echoing through the house. I'm in every New Year's Eve when the clock strikes midnight, and you're standing there, ready to face another year.

I'm holding your hand, just like you always held mine.

I love you, Maddy. More than words, more than time, more than life.

Always,
— Eve

By the time Maddy reached the end, her tears blurred the ink, smudging the familiar handwriting she had known all her life. She pressed the letter to her chest, feeling the weight of Eve's words settle into the cracks of her broken heart.

The world around her was silent, the snow falling in soft, steady waves, blanketing the night in a kind of quiet that felt both comforting and unbearable. She closed her eyes, letting herself feel the ache of Eve's absence, the warmth of her presence, the impossible, beautiful contradiction of loving someone who was no longer here.

And as the distant sound of fireworks echoed through the night, lighting up the sky with bright, fleeting bursts of colour, Maddy whispered into the stillness, her voice soft but steady.

"I love you too, Eve. Always."

And somehow, she knew Eve heard her.

I'm in the quiet mornings when the world is just waking up. I'm in the first snowfall of the year, in the smell of fresh coffee and old books, in the sound of your boys' laughter echoing through the house. I'm in every New Year's Eve when the clock strikes midnight, and you're standing there, ready to face another year.

I'm holding your hand, just like you always held mine.

I love you, Maddy. More than words, more than time, more than life.

Always,
– Eve

By the time Maddy reached the end, her tears blurred the ink, smudging the familiar handwriting she had known all her life. She pressed the letter to her chest, feeling the weight of Eve's words settle into the cracks of her broken heart.

The world around her was silent, the snow falling in soft, steady waves, blanketing the night in a kind of quiet that felt both comforting and unbearable. She closed her eyes, letting herself feel the ache of Eve's absence, the warmth of her presence, the impossible, beautiful contradiction of loving someone who was no longer here.

And as the distant sound of fireworks echoed through the night, lighting up the sky with bright, fleeting bursts of colour, Maddy whispered into the stillness, her voice soft but steady.

"I love you too, Eve. Always."

And somehow, she knew Eve heard her.

Maddy sat there for what felt like a long time, the letter trembling in her hands, her breath coming in slow, uneven waves. The ink had blurred where her tears had fallen, but it didn't matter. She knew every word would be seared into her heart forever, carved into the deepest parts of her in a way nothing could ever erase.

The snow kept falling, silent and steady, blanketing the world in something soft and endless. Somewhere in the distance, the last of the fireworks fizzled into the night, their fleeting brilliance already fading.

Maddy traced the loops of Eve's signature with her fingertips, her lips parting as if to say something, as if Eve could still hear her. But there were no words big enough, no language that could bridge the impossible space between them.

So instead, Maddy simply held the letter to her chest, her arms wrapped around it like she could somehow hold Eve too.

The cold bit at her skin, but she didn't move. Not yet.

Because for just a little while longer, she wanted to sit here, in the quiet, in the snow, in the last place she had ever sat with Eve on a night like this. She wanted to hold on to her best friend's words before time had the chance to make them feel distant.

She wanted to hold on to the memories.

Just a little longer.

Glitter, Candle Wax And Fate
New Years ~ 22 Years Ago

The apartment smelled like stale champagne, melted candle wax, and the last traces of laughter from the night before. The early afternoon light spilled through the half-covered windows, illuminating the evidence of their first real New Year's Eve in their own place—their *own* place.

Maddy stood barefoot in the middle of the living room, rubbing her temples, her head pounding from a hangover that had overstayed its welcome. Glitter—so much glitter—was scattered across the hardwood floors, catching the sunlight in tiny, mocking twinkles. The cheap pillar candles they had carefully arranged were now melted into uneven pools of wax, their bright colours staining the hardwood floor in pinks, blues, and golds.

Maddy bent down, picking up one of the many Polaroid pictures scattered across the room. The photo was slightly overexposed, but she could still make out Eve in the centre, laughing mid-toast, her plastic champagne glass raised high, surrounded by their friends. A perfect moment, frozen in time.

Eve groaned from across the room, crouched in the empty space where a couch should have been. "I think we underestimated how much wax would drip onto the floor." She peeled off a hardened clump, wincing as it flaked apart in her hands.

Maddy chuckled, moving to gather empty bottles into a trash bag. "We also underestimated how much glitter sticks to everything. We're gonna be finding this for years."

Eve snorted. "It's our apartment's new permanent feature." She straightened, rubbing her lower back, then eyed the mess around them. "Okay, let's divide and conquer. You take bottles and glasses, I'll tackle the wax and glitter. But not before we acknowledge what an absolutely iconic party that was."

Maddy smirked. "I'll admit, for two girls from Jim Thorpe with no furniture, we pulled it off."

They both laughed, the sound dissolving into comfortable silence as they continued cleaning. The faint sound of traffic drifted in from the street below, along with the occasional voice. The city was waking up slowly, shaking off its own hangover from the New Year's Eve celebrations.

Maddy glanced over at Eve, watching as she carefully peeled wax from the floor with a butter knife. Her best friend was quiet, which wasn't unusual, but there was a weight to it this morning.

"Hey." Maddy tossed an empty champagne bottle into the trash with a loud clink and leaned against the counter. "You okay?"

Eve looked up, lips pressing into a sheepish smile. "Yeah. Just… thinking about last night."

Maddy smirked. "About the party?"

Eve huffed out a laugh. "About me at the party."

Maddy grinned. "Ohhh. You mean how you drank way too much and ran off into the night like some tragic poet before I had to track you down?"

Eve groaned, flopping onto the floor dramatically. "God, don't remind me."

"I will remind you." Maddy crossed her arms. "You just left. One minute we were screaming the countdown, and the next, you were gone."

Eve groaned louder. "I thought I was going to be sick!"

"In an alley, Eve. You left the apartment and wandered into an alleyway in Bethlehem, a city we barely know. Who does that?"

Eve lifted her head. "Apparently me."

Maddy laughed, shaking her head. "I was so pissed. I had to throw on your coat over my dress and go looking for you like some stressed-out parent." She grabbed another Polaroid from the floor and turned it toward Eve. "See? Proof. This is you, looking all pathetic, sitting on the ground when I finally chased you down."

Eve took the photo, eyes narrowing at the slightly blurry image of herself, makeup smudged, wrapped in Maddy's scarf. She chuckled. "Wow. I was a mess."

Maddy flopped down beside her. "You were. But to be fair, you were also so dramatic about it. *Maddy, I think I'm lost forever. This might be where I die.*' You were literally in the alley behind the building, but lost forever!" Maddy laughed.

Eve buried her face in her hands. "Noooo." Her face reddened, but she laughed along with Maddy, knowing her friend wouldn't judge her.

"Oh, yes," Maddy said smugly. "And then, five minutes later, you were sobbing on my shoulder about how much you love me and how I'm your *forever person*."

Eve peeked through her fingers. "I mean… that part is true."

Maddy grinned, nudging Eve's shoulder with hers. "Obviously."

They sat there for a moment, surrounded by the wreckage of their first real celebration, the weight of the previous night still lingering in their bones.

Then Eve sighed dramatically. "Okay, we need coffee."

Maddy groaned. "Do we have coffee?"

Eve grimaced. "No."

They exchanged a look.

"The café down the street?" Maddy suggested.

Eve nodded solemnly. "We might die walking there, but it's a sacrifice we have to make."

Maddy snorted. "Let's go."

With their hangovers clinging to them, the little café on the corner felt like a million miles away, but they bravely made the trek. When they arrived, the café was packed with exhausted people trying to recover from their own nights of bad decisions. The smell of espresso and warm pastries wrapped around them as they stepped inside, the bell above the door chiming softly.

Eve was still clutching a Polaroid in her hand—one of them, from the night before, mid-laughter, arms around each other. Maddy rolled her eyes. "You're so sentimental."

Eve smirked. "Let me have my moment."

They shuffled forward in line, Eve still groaning occasionally about her headache. Maddy nudged her. "You're about to feel so much better. Coffee is magic."

Eve grumbled. "I need magic to fix me."

And then, she saw him.

Behind the counter, sleeves rolled up, hair just messy enough to look like he hadn't tried—but God, it worked. His eyes were a ridiculous shade of warm brown, the kind that made you forget how to function.

He laughed at something his coworker said, and it was so unfair. He was gorgeous.

Maddy followed Eve's gaze, then smirked. "Oh. Well. Hello, handsome."

Eve blinked. "What?"

Maddy grinned. "That's your future husband."

Eve snorted. "You're insane."

Maddy pushed her forward just as they reached the front of the line.

Sebastian turned to take her order, and Eve panicked. "I'll have... uhh...

your strongest coffee."

She paused.

Then, before she could stop herself—

"And maybe... your number?"

There was a horrible pause.

And then—he laughed. Not in a mean way. Not even in a surprised way. It was warm. Easy.

He scribbled something on her coffee cup before handing it over. "If you survive your hangover, text me." Next to the note was the name, Sebastian.

Eve gaped. Maddy nearly exploded from holding back her laughter.

As they walked out, Eve stared at the number scrawled on the cup.

Maddy bumped her shoulder. "Told you."

Eve shook her head, grinning despite herself. "Shut up."

Back in the present, back where Eve's spirit hung in the air, but Eve herself was nowhere, sitting out on the porch swing, Maddy smiled at the memory. In her mind, she pictured the framed polaroid she still kept at Once Upon A Latte. The one of Eve with her plastic champagne glass raised.

She could still hear Eve's laugh, still see the way her eyes had lit up when she walked out of that café, coffee in one hand, phone number in the other.

That had been the start of everything. Sebastian was the man Eve would marry. Maddy would be her maid of honour, dressed in a beautiful sky-blue gown.

And God, Maddy missed Eve.

Maddy inhaled deeply, exhaling into the cold air. The snow continued to fall, quiet and steady, wrapping the world in white.

She held onto the memory for just a little while longer.

A Long Road Home
New Years ~ 12 Years Ago

The party shimmered in gold and champagne, a living, breathing thing pulsing with music and motion. The vaulted ceilings stretched high above them, draped in strings of twinkling lights that flickered like fireflies in the dim glow. A massive projection of a countdown clock illuminated the far wall, the seconds ticking away as laughter and conversation swelled around it, rising and falling in time with the deep bass thrum of the music.

Everywhere, there was movement. Couples pressed close on the dance floor, swaying beneath the chandeliers, their sequined dresses and silk ties catching the light in dazzling bursts. Waiters weaved through the crowd, trays balanced with bubbling champagne flutes and delicate hors d'oeuvres. The scent of something warm and sweet—cinnamon, vanilla, maybe the remnants of dessert from the buffet—hung in the air, mixing with expensive colognes, perfumes, and the sharp bite of winter that slipped in each time the doors opened to welcome another late arrival.

Maddy stood near the bar, cradling a flute of champagne, her head tipped back in laughter as Derrick spun the stem of his empty glass between his fingers, grinning at some inside joke between them. He was warm from the alcohol, his tie already loosened, his dark hair slightly mussed from where Maddy had run her fingers through it. It was rare to see him this carefree, this light since Ben was born and they had become parents.

Across the room, Eve and Sebastian stood together, Eve's green dress catching the glow of the overhead lights, the colour making her eyes shine impossibly bright. She looked beautiful—God, she always looked beautiful—but Maddy could see the tension in her shoulders, the way she clutched her champagne flute just a little too tightly, the way she kept sneaking glances toward the entrance, toward her.

Maddy didn't have to ask why.

Sebastian had noticed Maddy's slight anxiety. He had noticed every time Maddy had checked her phone, every time she had stepped away to take a call from her mom, every time she had reassured herself that Ben was okay.

And Maddy had noticed something, too. Every time Maddy stepped away, Sebastian looked toward Eve, expectantly, and with something bordering on resentment.

Maddy turned slightly, just enough to see the way his jaw clenched, the way his fingers curled into a fist before he flexed them out again, as if trying to shake off whatever storm was building inside of him. He wasn't drinking anymore, though his glass was still in his hand. He wasn't laughing.

And when Maddy's phone buzzed again—just a short vibration, nothing urgent—she saw the moment it tipped something inside him.

Sebastian turned to Eve, and even over the noise, even from across the room, Maddy felt the change in the air.

The party was still shimmering, still golden, still alive with the thrill of a year coming to an end. But for Eve and Sebastian, something else was beginning. And it wasn't a celebration.

Maddy watched from across the room as Sebastian's posture stiffened, his hands curling into tight fists at his sides. His expression was a storm—

frustration, hurt, something even deeper churning beneath the surface. Eve stood in front of him, blinking rapidly, her eyes already glassy with unshed tears.

Maddy didn't have to hear their conversation to know what was happening. Her stomach twisted as she took in the way Sebastian's expression hardened, his frustration spilling into the sharp set of his jaw, the tightness in his fists. He was animated now, his hands moving in clipped gestures as he spoke, his voice just low enough that Maddy couldn't hear him over the hum of the party, but she didn't need to.

She knew what he was saying.

She had known this fight was coming.

Eve had been bracing for it for months, confiding in Maddy late into the night, voicing the fears she barely dared to admit even to herself. That Sebastian had already waited too long. That their timelines had never truly aligned the way they thought they would.

When they got married at 21, after two years together, they had talked about children like it was a certainty, a shared vision, a future they both wanted. But where Eve had imagined someday—after Sebastian finished medical school, after she got her master's degree in business—Sebastian had imagined *soon*. As in, *their honeymoon soon*.

Eve had managed to keep him waiting, first with school, then with the dream she and Maddy had built together—Once Upon A Latte. The coffee shop and bookstore had been everything they had ever wanted, a vision crafted over decades of friendship, late-night whispers, and childhood promises. It had taken everything they had to make it real. Eve had fought for it, poured herself into it, refused to let anything—*even love*—slow her down.

And then Maddy got pregnant.

It had been unexpected, unplanned, but Derrick had been thrilled. Maddy, terrified. But they had figured it out together, balancing their dreams of business ownership with the reality of raising a baby.

Sebastian hadn't understood why he and Eve couldn't do the same. He couldn't grasp why Eve, who had spent years saying *not yet*, still wasn't ready.

Maddy had been there for every whispered confession, every tearful *I don't know what to do*.

For every time Eve had admitted she was terrified—not just of losing her independence, not just of disrupting the trajectory she had spent years carving out for herself—but of becoming *her mother*.

Eve had always felt like an interruption in her mother's life, like a roadblock between her mother and the future she had once dreamed of. She had spent her childhood absorbing that unspoken resentment, and no matter how much she tried to push it down, she feared she would repeat the same cycle. She couldn't bring a child into the world with that doubt in her heart, and she had told Maddy, over and over again, that she wouldn't *risk* it.

But Sebastian didn't see it that way.

To him, she was *choosing* their business over their family. Choosing to wait for something she might never truly feel *ready* for.

Maddy didn't need to hear their words to know that's what this fight was about.

She saw it in the way Sebastian's hands curled into fists at his sides, in the way Eve wiped at her cheeks, already crying.

Sebastian gestured sharply with one hand, his mouth moving faster now, his words coming out too quick, too forceful. Eve's lips trembled as she tried to respond, but whatever she said only made Sebastian shake his head, his jaw tightening as he ran a hand through his hair, turning away from her for half a second before spinning back.

Maddy's chest ached at the sight of it—the widening gap between them, the silent plea in Eve's expression, the way Sebastian's frustration was morphing into something dangerously close to resignation.

Maddy's phone buzzed in her palm.

She glanced down. *Mom.*

She hesitated only for a second before she moved, slipping past the edges of the party, brushing Eve's shoulder as she passed. It was a silent promise—*I'm here. I see you. I'll be back.*

Eve barely turned, but Maddy felt her lean into the touch, just for a moment.

She stepped outside, the cold air biting at her skin, her breath puffing in soft clouds as she pressed the phone to her ear.

"Hey, Mom—"

But before she could even finish, the door swung open again, and Sebastian stormed past, his coat barely thrown over his arm as he strode toward the curb.

Maddy turned just in time to see the tension in his shoulders, the rigid set of his jaw, the way his breath came too sharp, too fast.

A taxi was already pulling up.

"Sebastian—" she started, but he didn't turn.

He yanked open the door, ducked inside, and just like that—he was gone.

Maddy pressed the phone closer to her ear, straining to hear her mother's voice over the faint static on the line.

"Ben has been crying for the last half hour," her mom said, concern lacing her words. "His fever is up again. I hate to call, but I think you should come home."

Maddy's stomach twisted. "Of course, Mom. We're on our way."

She turned on her heel, stepping quickly back into the bar, her heartbeat a sharp, anxious rhythm against her ribs. The room felt even warmer now, the low hum of conversation, the glint of champagne glasses, the golden glow of fairy lights all pressing in around her.

Derrick met her at the door, his brows furrowed. "What's wrong?"

"It's Ben," she said quickly. "His fever spiked. My mom says he won't settle—he's been crying. Mom thinks we should come and pick him up."

Derrick's expression shifted immediately, concern replacing the ease he had worn all night. He reached for his coat. "We should go."

Maddy hesitated, glancing past him toward the back of the bar, where the door to the women's bathroom was still slightly ajar. "Eve—"

Derrick followed her gaze, understanding passing between them instantly. "She went in there after Sebastian left," he murmured. "She hasn't come out."

Maddy clenched her jaw. She knew she needed to be with Ben, but she also knew Eve. If she was still in there, it meant she was barely holding herself together.

Derrick exhaled, already shrugging into his coat. "Go to her," he said gently. "I'll take a cab home and get Ben."

Maddy hesitated. "Are you sure?"

He nodded, pressing a reassuring hand to her shoulder. "You'd be thinking about her the whole time anyway. I've got Ben—go to Eve."

Relief flooded her. She squeezed Derrick's hand in silent gratitude before stepping away, weaving through the crowd toward the restroom.

She knocked gently. "Eve?"

Silence.

Maddy tried the handle—it turned easily.

Inside, the dim glow of the overhead light cast long shadows against the tiled walls. Eve was sitting on the closed toilet lid, her elbows resting on her knees, hands gripping her hair.

She looked up at Maddy, her eyes red, her mascara smudged. "He left," she whispered.

Maddy knelt in front of her, taking her hands. "I know."

Maddy crouched beside her, reaching out, tucking a strand of dark hair behind Eve's ear. "Hey," she murmured, her voice as steady as she could make it. "Talk to me."

Eve let out a broken laugh, wiping at her face with shaking hands. "What's there to say?" Her voice was raw, exhausted. "I told him I wasn't ready. That I still wanted more time. And he—he just left." She let out a hollow breath. "Not just the party, Maddy. I think he's done. I think he's going to ask me to move out."

Maddy frowned, her heart twisting at the sheer defeat in Eve's voice. "No, he's not."

"You don't know that." Eve protested. "I also told him it's not just that I'm not ready. I know that you are never truly ready," Eve swiped at the tears under her eyes. "I just," she stammered, "I just don't want it right now." She confessed. "I told him that. That's what I said right before he left."

"I do know he won't leave you," Maddy's voice was firm. She wasn't saying it to placate Eve—she meant it. She had seen the way Sebastian looked at

Eve in every room they were ever in. "Eve, that man worships you. He can't take his eyes off you, no matter where you are. And when he's not looking at you? He's thinking about you. He'd wait for you forever."

Eve let out a shuddering breath. "I don't know if that's true anymore."

Maddy cupped her face gently, forcing Eve to meet her gaze. "It is. I promise you, it is. He just... he's had too much to drink, and he let himself get caught up in all the what-ifs tonight. But that's all it is—a bad night." She softened, brushing her thumbs against Eve's damp cheeks, wiping away a smudge of mascara. "Come on. Let's get out of here."

Eve hesitated, but Maddy didn't give her a choice. She stood, holding out her hand. "I called a taxi. Let's go home."

Eve sniffled, taking Maddy's hand. "You don't have to come with me."

Maddy snorted. "Please. Like I'd let you walk into that house alone tonight."

The city lights blurred through the taxi window, streaking against the glass as the car wound its way through the quiet streets. Inside, the cab smelled faintly of citrus and worn leather, the radio playing something soft and old, a song neither of them recognized.

Maddy held Eve's hand, their fingers loosely laced together, a silent, steady comfort.

Eve exhaled shakily. "He's going to leave me."

Maddy squeezed her hand. Once. Twice. "He's not." She wished she could offer Eve more reassurance than a squeezed hand.

Eve let out a breathy laugh. "Of course he is," she protested. "I don't blame him."

"Stop it," Maddy turned her head, watching as Eve stared down at their joined hands, lost in the rise and fall of their entwined fingers. "Eve, if he wanted to leave, he would have done it a long time ago. He's still here."

Eve bit her lip, her chest rising and falling in uneven waves. "I just… I don't want to hold him back."

Maddy shook her head. "You're not."

Eve let out a sharp breath, squeezing her eyes shut. "Then why does it feel like I am?"

Maddy didn't answer right away. Instead, she squeezed Eve's hand again, three times, the same way they always had since they were kids. A quiet, unspoken promise.

I'm here. I see you. I'm not going anywhere.

Eve inhaled deeply, then slowly opened her eyes. The cab turned onto her street, the familiar silhouette of her home coming into view. But something about it made her breath hitch.

The lights were still on.

Through the upstairs window, she could see Sebastian moving inside, pacing through one of the spare bedrooms—the one next to theirs.

The one they always talked about turning into a nursery. They would paint it yellow when Eve was finally ready and she was pregnant.

At the sight of Sebastian, Eve's pulse quickened, her fingers tightening around Maddy's.

Maddy followed her gaze, then leaned in, whispering just loud enough to be heard. "He's waiting for you."

Eve swallowed. "I don't know if I can go inside."

Maddy turned to her fully, her voice steady. "Then I'll go with you. I'm here," she reassured Eve.

Eve exhaled shakily, nodding once as the taxi pulled to a stop.

Maddy turned to the cab driver. "Can you wait here? At least one of us—probably just me—will be coming back."

The driver nodded, adjusting the meter.

Maddy turned back to Eve, her voice steady. "Come on. Let's go see."

The cold night air pressed against them as they stepped out of the cab, the crisp scent of snow lingering in the quiet street. The soft glow from the front windows of Eve and Sebastian's home spilled onto the walkway, illuminating the path as they approached the door.

Maddy stayed close, her shoulder brushing against Eve's as they walked, her presence a silent reassurance. Eve's hands trembled as she reached for her keys, the jingle barely audible over the pounding of her heart.

She hesitated.

Maddy gently touched her back. "You've got this."

Eve exhaled, nodding. With a deep breath, she unlocked the door and pushed it open. The second it swung inward, Sebastian was there, breathless from a sprint down the stairs to the front door.

He pulled Eve into his arms so quickly, so fiercely, that she barely had time to breathe before she was enveloped in warmth, in the familiarness of him. His grip was desperate, his face buried in her hair, his breath coming in uneven, broken exhales.

"I'm sorry," he whispered, over and over again, the words tumbling out between shaky breaths. "God, Eve, I'm so sorry. I love you—I love you so much. I don't care about anything else. Not the timing, not the plans, not any of it." He cupped her face, his forehead pressing against hers as his voice dropped to a hoarse whisper. "You are what matters. Just you."

Eve let out a sob, her fingers curling into the fabric of his dress shirt, holding on like he was the only thing keeping her upright. "I don't want to lose you," she choked out.

Sebastian shook his head, his lips brushing against her forehead, her temple, her cheeks—anywhere he could reach. "You won't. You never could." He exhaled, a watery laugh slipping through his breath. "If you never want kids, if you're never ready, I don't care. We'll turn the spare bedrooms into a gym. Or a library. Or a shrine to your ridiculous coffee addiction."

Eve let out a broken laugh, half a sob, half a breath of relief, and buried herself against his chest.

Maddy turned and walked back down the path, her boots crunching softly against the snow. As she reached the curb, the taxi still waiting for her, she heard hurried footsteps behind her.

Then, suddenly, arms wrapped around her from behind. Eve.

Maddy barely had time to react before Eve squeezed her tightly, her cheek pressing against Maddy's shoulder.

"Happy New Year," Eve whispered.

Maddy swallowed the lump in her throat, placing her hands over Eve's. "Happy New Year," she said back.

Eve squeezed one last time before stepping back, her eyes shining as she turned and rushed back toward the house—toward Sebastian, toward their life, toward everything that was still waiting for her.

Maddy watched until the door closed behind her.

Then, with a deep breath, she climbed into the cab.

Now, Maddy sat on the porch swing, the cold air biting at her skin, the weight of memory pressing deep into her ribs. The snow had slowed, drifting lazily through the early morning air, the world around her hushed, still.

She ran her fingers over the edges of Eve's letter, her breath curling in soft clouds in the quiet of the early morning. For the first time since Eve had passed, Maddy didn't just feel the absence of her best friend.

She felt her presence.

In the words on the page. In the memory of laughter, of whispered secrets, of New Year's Eves spent side by side. In the way the night wrapped around her, gentle and familiar, as if Eve was still here, still holding on, still promising—I'm with you.

Maddy closed her eyes and let herself believe it.

A New Kind Of Celebration
New Years ~ 3 Years Ago

Maddy and Derrick's home smelled like vanilla, cinnamon, and freshly brewed coffee—the warm, familiar scents of comfort and home. In the corner of the living room, the Christmas tree still stood tall, its branches adorned with mismatched ornaments made by their two sons, Ben and Liam. The twinkle lights wrapped around it cast soft, golden patterns onto the hardwood floor, flickering like tiny, suspended stars.

Outside, snow fell steadily, thick flakes drifting through the cold Bethlehem night. The street beyond the frosted windows lay quiet, covered in a pristine, unbroken layer of white. Only the faint hum of the occasional car passing on the next street over interrupted the silence.

It was a far cry from the glittering, champagne-drenched New Year's Eve parties of Maddy and Eve's twenties and thirties. No sequined dresses or crowded dance floors. No thumping music or clinking glasses raised toward the ceiling in tipsy celebration. Tonight was slower, quieter—a night built around love, memory, and the steady, unshakable foundation of family.

Maddy shifted on the couch, grimacing slightly as the baby pressed against her ribs. At eight months pregnant, there were few positions that felt comfortable anymore, but tonight she didn't mind. She ran her hand absently over her swollen belly, feeling the faint ripple of movement beneath her palm. The baby was restless tonight, seemingly eager to join the world.

Across the room, Eve sat curled in an armchair by the fireplace, wrapped in a thick knit blanket, her body half-buried beneath its weight. Her legs were tucked beneath her, her feet hidden beneath the oversized wool. Her fingers played with the corner of the blanket as she watched Ben and Liam playing near the tree.

She had grown so much smaller since her diagnosis and the ensuing treatment.

The chemotherapy had hollowed her out in ways that still made Maddy's chest ache if she thought about it too long. Eve had always been petite, but the cancer treatments had stripped her of her soft curves. Her skin, once glowing and golden with warmth, had turned pale and almost translucent, the blue veins visible beneath the delicate surface. Her thick, dark hair had begun to grow back after the surgery—a soft, uneven crop of curls that framed her face like a halo of charcoal silk.

Maddy remembered the night Eve had first run her fingers through those curls, standing in front of the bathroom mirror, tears streaming down her cheeks. "I don't even look like me anymore," she had whispered.

Maddy had stood beside her, their reflections side-by-side, and smiled softly. "You look like you to me."

Now, watching Eve smiled with a contented sigh, Maddy saw the truth of those words again. The body might have changed, but the essence of her best friend remained unshaken.

"Stop it," Eve said without looking up.

Maddy blinked. "Stop what?"

"Staring at me like I might break at any second." Eve lifted a brow, a shadow of her old sass slipping through the exhaustion. "I swear, if you ask me one more time if I need anything, I will throw this blanket at you."

Maddy chuckled, lifting her hands in surrender. "I wasn't going to ask."

"Uh-huh." Eve narrowed her eyes, but there was warmth beneath the teasing. "I'm okay, Maddy. I mean it." She continued playing with the corner of the blanket as she settled deeper into the chair. "I'm not made of glass."

Maddy's smile softened. "No," she agreed, "you're made of steel." And she meant it—every word. So did everyone else in the room. They didn't just say it to soothe or comfort; they believed it, wholeheartedly, with the kind of conviction that left no room for doubt. Because imagining anything else—imagining a world without Eve's laughter, her warmth, her steady presence—was a heartbreak too vast to bear.

The faint clink of mugs interrupted their conversation. Sebastian and Derrick made their way from the kitchen, balancing a tray of steaming drinks, his expression one of exaggerated concentration as he stepped across the room into the living room.

"Alright, listen," he said, voice low with mock seriousness. "We've followed the instructions we were given exactly. We've got one peppermint tea for the pregnant lady, one hot chocolate with an unreasonable amount of whipped cream for my beautiful wife, and—" he paused, turning as to Derrick. "—one normal person's hot chocolate for me and a Bailey's for Derrick."

Derrick grinned as Sebastian handed him the tumbler of cream-laced liqueur. "You're a good man," Derrick said, clinking his glass against Sebastian's mug.

"I'm an excellent man," Sebastian agreed with a proud smile.

Eve smirked, eyeing the towering swirl of whipped cream on her cocoa. "I'm impressed. I figured you'd just get distracted halfway through and forget what I asked for."

Sebastian pressed a hand to his chest, staggering back a step. "Wounded. Deeply wounded."

Eve rolled her eyes, but she was smiling. When Sebastian bent to kiss her forehead, she leaned into him, her eyes fluttering shut for a moment.

Maddy's throat tightened at the sight.

Maddy's gaze lingered on the way Sebastian's hand rested gently on Eve's knee, his thumb tracing slow, absent-minded circles over the soft knit of the blanket. The touch was instinctive—habitual, protective. And yet, even now, months after Eve's diagnosis, Maddy couldn't forget how hard it had been for her best friend to accept that kind of care from him.

The night Eve told Sebastian she had cancer was still etched into Maddy's memory, not because she had been there, but because Eve had called her afterward, sobbing so hard she could barely get the words out. It had taken her hours to work up the courage to say it out loud to him. Not because she doubted his love—but because letting him in meant letting someone take care of her. Eve had always been the caretaker—in her marriage, in her friendships, in nearly every corner of her life. It was how she showed her love, how she made sense of the world.

Maddy knew this better than anyone. And so, she worked hard to be the one person Eve didn't have to take care of. The one who showed up, who carried the weight when Eve needed it most, even when she didn't ask.

Eve had always been the fixer, the watchman, the one who smoothed over problems and made everyone else feel safe. The idea of becoming someone who needed care had shaken her to her core. She hadn't known how to lean on Sebastian—not when leaning meant confronting her own fear and helplessness.

Maddy remembered Eve's voice on the other end of the line that night, cracked and brittle: "He cried, Maddy. He just... held me and cried. I didn't think I could survive telling him."

And yet, Eve had.

She had told him. And Sebastian had shown up—not just in words, but in every way that mattered. For every appointment, every infusion, every surgery.

Even when Eve had tried to downplay the pain, smiling through clenched teeth and insisting she was fine. Even when she'd told Sebastian she could handle the nausea, the fatigue, the unrelenting weight of it all on her own. He had been there—his hand wrapped firmly around hers through every brutal, bone-deep moment.

And now, watching them here, sitting side-by-side, Sebastian perched on the stone hearth of the fireplace, Maddy saw that same quiet devotion woven into every touch, every glance. The fire crackled softly behind them, its amber glow dancing across their faces, while the boys played near the tree with toys they'd unwrapped just a week earlier, their laughter bright and unburdened.

Maddy smiled, setting her mug on the coffee table with a soft clink. She clapped her hands together. "Okay! I have a surprise."

Eve sat up a little straighter, curiosity lighting her face. "Should I be scared?"

"Probably." Maddy grinned, reaching beside the couch and pulling out a clunky, scuffed Polaroid camera. "Ta-da!"

Eve's eyes widened as she pushed the blanket aside and sat up so quickly Sebastian had to steady her arm. "No way."

"The one and only," Maddy declared proudly. "Dug it out of storage and managed to track down some film on eBay. I thought we could recreate our first apartment New Year's Eve—minus the alley incident."

Eve groaned, her head falling back against the chair. "I'm never going to live that down, am I?" She laughed, sitting up again. "And I sincerely hope we're leaving the glitter where it belongs—as a cautionary tale buried deep in the past. I swear, I still find random flecks in my hair."

Maddy smirked. "No, you'll never live it down. And absolutely no glitter this year, or ever again."

Sebastian and Derrick exchanged amused glances.

"Should we know what you're both talking about?" Sebastian asked, leaning forward with a raised eyebrow.

Maddy bit back a laugh. "Let's just say your wife has... a colourful history."

"It's true," Eve said, shrugging unapologetically. "But if that ridiculous night hadn't happened, I never would have met Sebastian." She turned to him then, her smile soft and radiant, and reached for his hand. He took it without hesitation, without needing to look.

"Okay, well, I don't think we need all the details," Sebastian said with a laugh. "But if some alleyway misadventure led you into that café that day, I'll call it a win."

Before either woman could respond, Ben and Liam froze mid-play, their attention locked on the camera in Maddy's hands.

"What is that?" Ben asked, eyes wide with fascination.

Maddy grinned, crouching beside them. "It's magic." She held the camera up. "This takes pictures, but instead of showing up on a screen, they print out right away."

"Like a printer?" Liam asked, his brow furrowed.

"Like *magic*," Maddy repeated, her voice dropping to a whisper for effect. The boys were instantly enthralled. Within minutes, they had completely monopolized the camera. The soft click-whirr of the Polaroid became a constant soundtrack as they raced around the room, snapping pictures of each other, their toys, the fireplace—and, inexplicably, their own feet.

Eve chuckled, leaning her head back against the chair. "I feel like we're not going to get any actual pictures of us tonight."

Maddy smiled, watching her sons tumble across the carpet in a blur of laughter and limbs. "That's okay."

Because tonight wasn't about perfect pictures. It wasn't about recapturing something from their past. It was about this moment. It was about all of the moments in between.

The laughter. The warmth. The mugs of hot chocolate and the scent of cinnamon and the sound of the boys squealing with delight every time the Polaroid spat out another picture. It was about the sight of Sebastian sitting beside Eve, his hand resting gently on her knee like it belonged there. About the way Derrick's eyes softened as he knelt beside Ben, showing him how to shake the Polaroid to develop the image faster, even though Maddy was pretty sure that trick had been debunked years ago.

It was about the way Eve's smile lingered when she thought no one was looking.

Maddy was full of fear—fear that this was their last New Year's Eve before the cancer would return. She pushed her thoughts aside. Tonight, there was only this. This night. This warmth. This love.

Maddy reached for the spare roll of film and loaded it into the camera. Then she held it up.

"Okay, everyone!" she called. "Picture time!"

Ben and Liam scrambled into place in front of where Eve sat. Sebastian knelt beside Eve, his arm wrapped protectively around her. Derrick settled behind Maddy, resting his hands on her shoulders.

The camera clicked.

The photo printed, the image slowly developing until their smiling faces emerged from the haze of chemicals and light.

Maddy held the photo between her fingers, the edges warm from her touch.

This moment—this memory—would last.

No matter what the future held.

Later, the clock on the mantel struck midnight, its soft chime cutting through the easy hum of conversation and the faint crackle of the fire. Outside, the snow fell in thick, steady sheets, blanketing the quiet street in soft white. Inside, the living room was cocooned in warmth—mugs resting on coasters, blankets draped over laps, and the remnants of laughter lingering like the echo of a cherished melody.

Ben and Liam stirred on the couch, roused by the familiar countdown blaring faintly from the television. Their eyes, heavy with sleep, fluttered open just in time to see the glowing numbers reach zero.

"Happy New Year!" Maddy called softly, her voice threading through the dimly lit room. She lifted her mug of peppermint tea, her smile wide despite the ache in her back and the weight of the baby pressing low against her ribs. Beside her, Derrick squeezed her hand with affection, his other arm slung across the back of the couch. Across the room, Eve grinned, her cheeks flushed from the heat of the fire, her mug of hot chocolate held high. Sebastian shifted closer to her, his arm resting along the back of her chair, his fingers idly brushing her shoulder.

The boys, roused for only a moment by the declaration of midnight, mumbled their own sleepy "Happy New Year" before collapsing once again into the pillows. The adults laughed softly at the sight of their tousled hair and slack expressions.

"Well," Derrick said, raising his glass to the others. "To the simplest, most wonderful New Year's Eve yet."

"To simplicity," Sebastian echoed, his voice low and sincere. He turned toward Eve, brushing a stray curl from her forehead. "And to having you here with us."

Eve's eyes softened as she met his gaze. "I wouldn't want to be anywhere else."

Maddy watched the moment unfold between them, the depth of their love as obvious as the flicker of the firelight on the walls. She thought back to all the nights they'd spent in hospitals over the last few month—waiting rooms, sterile hallways, and the hum of infusion pumps that seemed to whisper fears they never dared voice aloud. The battle had been brutal. Ovarian cancer didn't fight fair. The diagnosis had come as winter set in. Surgery had come first—a total hysterectomy, followed by chemotherapy. Maddy remembered sitting beside Eve in the hospital, reading aloud from their favourite childhood books while the IV dripped slow poison into her veins. The side effects had been merciless—nausea, weakness, hair loss, and a fatigue that clung to Eve's bones long after the treatments ended. But through it all, she had smiled. Laughed. Fought. And now, though her body bore the marks of that battle, her spirit remained unchanged.

Eve caught Maddy watching her and arched an eyebrow. "You're doing it again."

Maddy blinked. "Doing what?"

"Looking at me like I might crack if you breathe too hard." Eve smirked, though her voice trembled with emotion. "I swear, I'm fine. Tired, yes. But fine."

Maddy's chest tightened. "I know. I just... I don't want to take a single minute for granted."

Eve reached across the space between them and squeezed her hand. "Neither do I." The fire crackled softly in the silence that followed, the warmth of the moment wrapping around them like a well-worn blanket.

The contraction came out of nowhere—a sudden, sharp tightening low in Maddy's abdomen. She gasped softly, instinctively pressing her hand against her belly.

Derrick's head whipped toward her. "Mads?"

She exhaled slowly, willing her muscles to relax. "I'm okay. It's just... a Braxton Hicks contraction. It's been happening off and on all day."

Eve frowned. "Are you sure?"

"Positive," Maddy said, though she wasn't entirely convinced. The tightening had felt different this time—sharper, more purposeful. But it passed, and she forced a smile to reassure them. "Come on. Let's take one more picture," Maddy suggested, holding up her Polaroid camera again.

Sebastian wrangled the boys into position near the tree while Derrick set the Polaroid on the coffee table and adjusted the focus. Maddy eased herself up from the couch with a soft groan, gripping Eve's outstretched hand for support. They stood side by side, their shoulders pressed together, smiling as the flash burst.

The photo slid from the camera with a soft whirr.

Eve plucked it from the tray and shook it gently, her eyes bright with nostalgia. "I forgot how much I love these."

The image slowly developed—two women standing side by side, their family all around them. One heavily pregnant, the other thinner than she should have been, both smiling with a kind of love that years, distance, and illness had only strengthened.

Maddy was still smiling when the second contraction hit.

This time, there was no mistaking it.

The pressure bore down on her lower back with an intensity that left her gasping. Her knees buckled slightly, and she grasped Eve's arm with both hands.

"Maddy?" Eve's voice sharpened with concern. "What's happening? Are you okay?"

The pain crested, then slowly ebbed, leaving Maddy breathless.

She locked eyes with Eve. "I think... I think it's happening."

Derrick swore softly and rushed toward her, sliding an arm around her waist. "Okay. Okay, let's get you to the hospital."

"I'll get the car," Sebastian said, already heading for the door.

Maddy shook her head. "No time. Call a cab."

Derrick pulled out his phone with trembling fingers.

Maddy leaned into Eve's side, breathing through the next contraction. "You're coming with me," she said between shallow breaths.

Eve's eyes widened. "Are you sure? Derrick—"

"Derrick needs to stay with the boys and… and get them to my mom's." Maddy squeezed her hand. "But I need you, Eve. I need you with me. You were there for Ben and Liam. I want you there for this one too!" She declared.

The taxi pulled up in front of the house just as another contraction hit.

Eve didn't hesitate. She wrapped an arm around Maddy's waist and guided her out into the snow. The boys stood by the window, their little faces pressed against the glass, watching with wide eyes as their mother was helped into the cab.

"Tell them I love them," Maddy whispered to Derrick.

"I will," he promised. He kissed her forehead, his lips lingering for half a second longer than usual. "Go have our baby. I'll meet you at the hospital."

Maddy nodded, then turned her face into Eve's shoulder as the cab doors closed.

The car jolted forward, the wheels crunching through the snow. The city blurred past the windows—dark streets lined with old brick houses, the occasional glow of a porch light breaking through the shadows. Inside the car, the heater hummed softly, the warm air contrasting with the cold fear building in Maddy's chest.

Eve's hand found hers. Their fingers intertwined—strong, steady, unbreakable.

The contractions came faster now. Maddy moaned softly, her body bowing beneath the force of the pain.

Eve tightened her grip. "You're doing so well, Maddy. Breathe with me." The fatigue that had been Eve's constant companion since her diagnosis had ebbed, giving her a burst of strength Eve was all too happy to shower upon her friend.

Maddy nodded, trying to match Eve's measured breaths.

As the car rounded a corner, the streetlights cast golden streaks across the glass. Maddy's head lolled against the window. "Eve," she whispered. "I'm scared. It's early." While this was Maddy's third child, it was the first time her baby had been early. Maddy's mind raced with thoughts of what delivering a baby at 36 weeks might mean.

Eve shifted closer, resting her forehead against Maddy's temple. "I know. But you're not alone. I'm here. I'll stay right here, no matter what."

Maddy's breath hitched. The next contraction stole her voice, but her fingers tightened around Eve's with desperate strength.

She squeezed once.

Twice.

Three times.

Eve's answering squeeze came immediately—three soft pulses of reassurance.

I'm here. I'm here. I'm here.

The taxi turned into the hospital's emergency entrance. The lights above the automatic doors glowed faintly against the snow-covered pavement.

The cab came to a stop, the meter ticking softly in the sudden silence.

Eve climbed out of the cab and rushed around to Maddy's side. She held Maddy by the elbow as she helped her out of the car and toward the emergency entrance of St Luke's University Hospital, the same hospital Sebastian worked at as a pediatric surgeon. The hospital doors slid open, releasing a gust of warm, antiseptic-scented air into the cold night.

Maddy clung to Eve as they stepped into the sterile light. From there, everything happened quickly.

A labour room was already prepped when they arrived. A nurse ushered them inside, barking orders for monitors and equipment.

Maddy lay back on the bed, her eyes squeezed shut, her breath coming in shallow gasps.

Eve never let go of her hand.

The pain blurred into something distant, dreamlike—a series of crashing waves she couldn't outrun. The room seemed to dissolve into watercolour shapes: the pale green of the walls, the silver glint of medical instruments, the deep blue of Eve's sweater. The contractions were fierce and unrelenting, driving her toward something inevitable and beautiful.

"Okay, Maddy," the doctor said. "It's time to push."

Maddy opened her eyes. "Eve—"

"I'm here," Eve whispered. "I'll stay, no matter what."

Maddy pushed. The world tilted, twisted, expanded. The pressure intensified, then broke.

The baby's cry sliced through the air. Even at 36 weeks, he was perfect.

A nurse placed the tiny, warm body against Maddy's chest. The baby's skin was flushed but strong, his lungs announcing his arrival with surprising strength. Maddy cradled the baby's head with trembling fingers. "Chester," she whispered.

Eve brushed Maddy's hair back from her forehead. "He's gorgeous," she said, her voice thick with emotion.

Maddy turned her head toward Eve, her face damp with sweat and relief. "Thank you," she murmured. "For being here. For everything."

Eve squeezed her hand, three times.

"I'll stay," she whispered. "I'll always stay."

Now, the memory of that years-ago New Years, and all the ones that came before, shimmered like frost beneath the present moment, clinging to Maddy's skin as the cold night air bit through her sweater. Eve's letter still pressed to her chest, her heart still racing with the weight of Eve's words. She could almost hear the echo of laughter from that glitter-streaked apartment, the way they'd sat side-by-side, sticky with candle wax and hope. Maddy's mind reeled with all the New Years celebrations in between.

But tonight, it was just her.

The creak of the back door jolted Maddy from the depths of memory, sharp and sudden against the quiet night. She turned to see Derrick stepping outside, his breath ghosting into the cold like a restless spirit. He lingered in the doorway for a moment, eyes searching hers as if he could sense the fragile thread tethering her to the present. Then, without a word, he crossed the porch and sat beside her, his presence crackling with unspoken questions and the weight of things unsaid.

"They asleep?" she asked, voice cracking through the silence.

Derrick nodded. "Out cold. Chester fought it, though. Kept asking for another story."

Maddy's lips curved into the faintest smile. "He always does."

They sat there for a moment, the snow falling in slow, lazy spirals around them. The yard was quiet, the only sounds the distant crackle of fireworks and the wind stirring the bare branches overhead.

Then Derrick shifted slightly, his arm brushing hers. "You want to tell me what Eve said in the letter?"

Maddy swallowed hard, the words tangled in her throat. She didn't want to break the spell of the letter, didn't want to translate Eve's voice into her own. But Derrick was here. Solid and real and waiting.

"She said... she's still with me," Maddy whispered, her breath fogging the cold air. "That every New Year's Eve, she'll be here. That she's in the little moments. The snow. The coffee. The boys' laughter." Her voice cracked. "That she's still holding my hand."

Derrick reached over and took her hand in his, his palm warm despite the cold. "She's right, you know," he said softly.

Maddy squeezed his hand, the tears slipping down her cheeks faster than she could wipe them away. "It just... hurts so much. It hurts to not be able to see her, to talk to her. To go to work every day and she's not there."

"I know." Derrick pulled Maddy closer, tucking her against his side. "But she knew what she was doing, waiting until tonight. She wanted you to remember that she's more than just the loss. She's everything that came before it, too."

Maddy closed her eyes, breathing in the crisp, clean scent of the snow. He was right. Eve had always loved New Year's Eve, not because of the countdown or the confetti, but because of the promise it held. The clean slate. The undeniable magic of stepping into something new while holding on to the memories of everything that came before.

The wind stirred the snow around their feet, swirling it into soft, glittering patterns against the dark. And as it passed, Maddy could have sworn she heard it—soft, faint, but unmistakable.

I'm here, Maddy.

Her heart clenched, and she sat up, releasing Derrick's hand. The cold bit harder now, like the universe itself was holding its breath.

"Did you hear that?" she asked.

Derrick frowned. "Hear what?"

Maddy scanned the yard, the trees, the street beyond. Nothing. Just snow and quiet. But the sensation lingered—Eve's presence, as if her best friend were sitting beside her once again, watching the snow fall like they always had.

The clock inside the house had long since gone silent, its chimes faded into the past along with the fireworks that had painted the sky. Midnight had come and gone, ushering in a new year without ceremony, without the shared laughter and whispered resolutions that had once defined this night.

Maddy stood, the letter still cradled in her hands, and drifted toward the edge of the porch. The snow cushioned her footsteps, muffling each step until it felt as though she were floating across a landscape untouched by time. The cold air scraped her throat with every breath, sharp and unforgiving, but she welcomed the sting. It was something she could feel—something real, here, now, when everything else seemed lost in the haze of memory.

Behind her, Derrick shifted, his boots crunching softly against the snow as he followed. He stopped a few steps away, silent but present, the warmth of his concern reaching for her like an invisible string.

Maddy's eyes lifted to the night sky. The stars shimmered through the thinning veil of snowfall, distant and indifferent. Her fingers tightened around the letter, the paper pliant and familiar beneath her touch.

The wind stirred without warning, sweeping down from the treetops with a hollow whisper that danced across the snow. It curled around her, lifting the edges of the letter, slipping beneath her hair, brushing her cheeks with a touch that felt impossibly familiar.

Her breath caught.

The wind shifted again, and this time the whisper was clearer.

Happy New Year, Maddy.

Her eyes stung with the sharpness of the sound—no louder than a sigh, but unmistakable. The voice she had thought she'd never hear again. The voice that had been with her through every scraped knee and heartbreak, every dream and disappointment. The voice that could make her laugh through tears, or soften the hardest truths with a single word.

Her knees wobbled, and she leaned into the porch railing, the cold wood biting into her palms. The letter trembled against her chest as she clutched it to her heart.

She wanted to turn to Derrick, to ask if he had heard it too. But some part of her already knew the answer.

This was for her.

Instead, when she turned to Derrick, she just whispered "I'll be inside in a few minutes," she words a gentle dismissal. "I just want to spend a few more minutes with it all."

Derrick nodded. His boots crunching through the freshly fallen snow marked his path as he headed back inside.

Alone again, the wind softened, swirling the snow into glittering spirals that danced across the porch steps. The cold pressed closer, but Maddy didn't move. She let the silence settle around her like a blanket, let the ache expand until it filled every hollow space left behind by Eve's absence.

Because some friendships don't fade. Some loves never leave.
And Eve—Eve had never really gone.

She was here. In every memory. In the quiet of the snow. In the hush of the new year. Maddy pressed her lips to the edge of the letter, her breath warming the cold paper. Her voice broke the silence, soft and steady despite the tremble in her chest.

The Weight Of Absence
New Years ~ Present Day

Maddy stood at the kitchen counter, absently running her fingers over the smooth quartz surface. The texture was familiar—warn from years of family breakfasts, sticky with memories of syrup spills and half-finished homework assignments. The evening air outside the window carried the distant crackle of fireworks from the city's early celebrations, but inside the house, the silence pressed against her chest like a weight she couldn't shake.

It was New Year's Eve.

Her favourite night of the year.

And Eve's, too.

Or it had been.

The ache of that thought settled deep in Maddy's chest as she reached for the cutting board and began slicing cheese for the charcuterie board she was working on. Sharp cheddar, creamy brie, tangy blue—all arranged with the kind of meticulous care that came with distraction rather than intention. The knife slid through the brie's soft centre too easily, the pressure unmeasured, the wedge collapsing beneath her grip.

"Damn it," she whispered, setting the knife aside.

Behind her, footsteps padded into the kitchen. She didn't need to turn around to know it was Derrick. He had a way of entering rooms with the quiet ease of someone who never needed to announce himself—just warmth arriving without ceremony.

"You okay?" he asked, his voice soft, but his eyes sharp as he leaned against the doorframe framing the entrance to their open plan kitchen and living room.

Maddy wiped her hands on her apron. "Yeah. Just... trying to get everything ready."

Derrick pushed off the frame and crossed to the kitchen, wrapping his arms around Maddy's waist from behind. His chin rested lightly on her shoulder, his breath warm against her neck. For a moment, she let herself lean into him, the solid presence of him grounding her.

"They don't care about the snacks, you know," he murmured. "The boys just want to stay up past their bedtime. And I just want you to stop grinding your teeth."

Maddy let out a weak laugh, but it caught halfway up her throat. "It's our first New Year's without her," she said quietly, voice cracking on the final word.

Derrick didn't respond with empty reassurances. He just held her tighter. Maddy closed her eyes, imagining the way Eve would've swooped into the kitchen right about now—complaining about the cold, demanding first dibs on the brie, and laughing about how bad they were at being grown-ups even after all these years.

But the brie was crumbled. And Eve wasn't coming.

Maddy placed the last piece of crumbled brie on the charcuterie board and stood back, assessing the uneven arrangement of cheeses, crackers, and sliced fruit. It didn't look right. The grapes sagged against the edge of

But Eve wasn't here. And no matter how Maddy tried to fill the spaces with crackers and cheese and wine glasses arranged just-so, the absence remained.

The clock on the oven read 6:42 p.m.

Sebastian would have been here by now.

She had invited him weeks ago—texted him one afternoon while sitting in the breakroom at Once Upon A Latte. *Come by for New Year's Eve. The boys would love to see you.* We'd love to see you. He never responded.

Maddy tried to tell herself she hadn't expected him to.

Since Eve's passing, Sebastian had drifted into silence. His leave of absence from the hospital had stretched out with no end in sight. Maddy had stopped by the house once, bringing soup and cinnamon rolls, hoping to coax him into conversation.

He hadn't answered the door.

She'd stood on the front step of the large house that had been his and Eve's dream home, for a long time that day, staring at the windows. The curtains were drawn, but the faintest crack of light glowed from the second floor—from the yellow room.

Her throat had tightened at the sight.

The yellow room. The one he and Eve had painted with hope and plans for the future—soft buttery walls meant for lullabies and bedtime stories, for beginnings, for family. Not endings.

Sebastian had been sleeping in there since she passed. Alone. In the room where their dreams had lived only in imagination and died the early morning Eve's heart went still. Maddy's heart clenched now at the memory.

"Mom, is Sebastian coming?" Liam asked from the living room, his voice tentative.

She forced a smile. "No, sweetheart. Not tonight."

"Why not?" Liam frowned. "He loves New Year's."

"He used to," Maddy said softly. "But it's hard for him this year."

Liam nodded, as if he understood more than she realized. "I miss Eve."
"Me too," Maddy whispered. "Every day."

Liam shuffled back to the living room, leaving Maddy standing at the kitchen counter with the broken brie and the weight of knowing Sebastian was out there—just a few streets away—alone in that empty yellow room.

The cold from the quartz countertop seeped into her palms. Maddy squeezed her eyes shut and took a deep breath, willing herself to release the thought of Sebastian and the unrelenting ache that had settled into her chest since Eve's passing. The grief was always there, just beneath the surface, like a sharp-edged stone beneath water. Some days, it cut her open. Other days, she could almost convince herself it had dulled.

Tonight, she wanted it to dull.

She wanted the boys to remember this night with laughter and warmth, the way Eve would have insisted. Eve had always said New Year's Eve wasn't about endings; it was about beginnings. A clean slate. A fresh page.

So Maddy forced her hands to move. She straightened the brie as best she could, repositioned the crackers, adjusted the grapes until they looked more intentional than defeated. The wine glasses caught the glow of the pendant lights above the kitchen island, casting fragile rainbows across the counter. She poured herself a glass of red wine and took a long, steadying sip before topping her glass and filling Derrick's.

The sound of the boys wrestling drifted over from the couch—thuds and giggles, protests and shrieks. Maddy let herself smile at the sounds of the lives she and Derrick had created together.

"Okay, okay," she called, stepping across the room. "No broken bones before midnight. That's the rule."

Ben tumbled off the couch in a fit of laughter, landing in a heap on the rug. Liam immediately sprawled across his back while Chester attempted to climb both of them like a human jungle gym, though he was much younger and smaller than his two older brothers.

Derrick looked up from where he sat on the couch, legs stretched out, one arm slung across the back. His gaze softened when it met hers. "Need help?"

Maddy set the charcuterie board on the coffee table and lowered herself onto the couch beside him. "I think I'm past saving." She handed Derrick his glass of wine.

Derrick chuckled and reached over, squeezing her knee. His hand lingered there—warm, steady, familiar. The weight of his touch felt like a reminder of happiness in a night that seemed determined to drift into sadness.

The boys attacked the board with the enthusiasm of children who had been promised a late bedtime and sugar-fuelled freedom. Maddy watched them, her chest tightening at the sight of Chester holding a cracker high in triumph before Liam stole it with a swipe of his hand. The living room crackled with life, but the shadows in the corners felt deeper tonight.

Eve should be here.

She should be sprawled on the floor with the boys, sneaking olives and rolling her eyes at Maddy's "too fancy" cheese choices. She should be laughing at the mess, talking about new beginnings.

Maddy's throat burned. She reached for her wine.

The evening stretched on. The boys played, shouted, and collapsed into fits of laughter. Maddy and Derrick curled together on the couch, half-watching movies and half-narrating scenes with increasingly ridiculous commentary—just as Eve used to do when the plotlines became too predictable.

By ten o'clock, Chester had fallen asleep on the rug, his cheeks flushed from excitement and exertion. Maddy draped a blanket over him, brushing his fine hair from his forehead.

Derrick was quiet behind her. When she turned, she found him watching her with an expression she couldn't quite name—tenderness, yes, but something else.

"What?" she asked softly.

"Nothing." His lips curved slightly. "Just... I know how hard tonight is for you."

Maddy swallowed. "Yeah."

His hand found hers. "She'd be proud of you."

The words landed like a blow and a balm all at once. Maddy squeezed his fingers, clinging to the warmth of his touch. "I just... I want to get it right. For the boys. For her."

"You already are." Derrick kissed the top of her head. "You always have." She leaned into him, closing her eyes against the ache of loss. Derrick's arm wrapped around her shoulders, and for a moment, the noise of the night faded, replaced by the sound of her heart beating against the raw edges of memory.

They stayed like that for a while. Maddy tried to let herself sink into the warmth of Derrick's body, the comfort of his steady breath, the faint scent of cedar and soap that had always made her feel safe. But the emptiness remained—there, in the corner of the room, where Eve would have stood with a glass of wine, narrating the boys' antics with childish and playful commentary and pretending she wasn't getting teary-eyed when they counted down to midnight.

It's not the same without you, Maddy thought.

And it never would be.

By eleven-thirty, Liam had passed out on the couch, and Ben was valiantly trying to keep his eyes open, blinking heavily as he lay with his head on

Derrick's leg. Maddy stood to stretch, her legs aching from hours of sitting in one position.

"Fresh air," she said to Derrick.

He nodded, his eyes following her as she stepped toward the back door.

Outside, the snow fell in soft, silent drifts. The night air bit at her cheeks, stealing the warmth from her skin as she crossed the deck to the porch swing. The wood creaked beneath her as she sat, drawing her knees to her chest and wrapping her arms around them.

The streetlights cast a faint glow across the snow-covered yard. A fresh blanket of snow covered the evidence of the boys playing outside earlier that day.

She remembered all the New Year's Eves when she and Eve had sat here together, wrapped in blankets, whispering their resolutions to the stars. Eve had vowed to learn how to bake something other than boxed brownies. Maddy had sworn she'd stop checking her phone every time she got a notification from Instagram, promising herself she'd be more present.

They had laughed, long and hard, until their cheeks hurt and their breaths came out in white clouds of shared joy.

Maddy shivered now, blinking against the sting in her eyes. The silence of the night pressed down around her, heavy and absolute.

Inside, Derrick was probably wondering what was taking her so long. With just 15-minutes left until the New Year, Derrick was probably waking the boys up from their sprawling sleep in a tangle of limbs and blankets.

She should go back in for midnight.

She would.

Just... not yet.

Maddy tilted her head back and stared at the stars, each one shimmering cold and distant against the black sky. Somewhere, across the neighbourhood, a firework cracked, its faint glow reflecting in the snow.

The wind shifted. Snowflakes swirled around her. The scent of pine and crisp night air filled her lungs.

Finally, just before midnight, she stepped back into her home, the warmth of the familiar walls doing little to thaw the cold lodged in her chest. She went through the motions of ringing in the New Year with her husband and boys—laughing when they laughed, smiling when they cheered—but every movement felt like walking through water, heavy and unsteady. Their joy was a lifeline she clung to, fleeting and fragile, easing the ache for a moment. Just a moment. But beneath it, the emptiness remained—a hollow, aching space where Eve should have been, where Eve still was, everywhere and nowhere, like the memory of a melody she could hum but never quite grasp.

*****

Now, with the New Year settling in, the cold wrapped around Maddy as she settled back onto the porch swing, the letter still pressed to her chest. The snow had thickened, the flakes growing heavier, swirling in the dim glow of the moonlight like tiny pieces of the past drifting through the night. Her breath formed soft clouds in the air, rising and vanishing as quickly as the moments she wished she could hold on to forever.

The quiet stretched on, vast and empty. Yet, somehow, not entirely.

She could feel Eve here, even now—woven into the night's silence, into the snowflakes that landed on her cheeks, into the faint scent of evergreen carried on the breeze. The past was never really gone. It clung to her in every memory, every inside joke that no one else would understand, every New Year when they had stood side-by-side, laughing at nothing and everything.

The ache in Maddy's chest tightened, sharp and piercing, but beneath it, there was something else. Something softer.

Love.

Not just the memory of it, but the presence of it. The kind that didn't leave with death, that stayed lodged in the invisible spaces of a life once shared. The kind of love Eve had promised in the letter—the kind that didn't end when the clocks struck midnight, when calendars changed, when hearts broke.

She traced the worn edges of the paper with her fingertips, the ink smudged beneath the press of her tears. Eve's words lingered there, etched into the fibres of the page and the marrow of Maddy's bones.

I'm still here, Maddy.

The wind stirred again, brushing across her skin like a whisper.

I'm here.

Maddy swallowed hard and looked up toward the sky. The stars shimmered through the snowfall, distant and endless. The constellations they'd tried to name as kids stretched out across the blackness. Eve had always made up her own names for them—*The Coffee Cup, The Unstoppable Duo, The Great Glitter Explosion*—and Maddy could still hear Eve's laughter as she pointed out shapes that didn't exist, making magic out of nothing.

Maddy exhaled, the sound shaky and broken.

"You really got me with this one, Eve," she whispered into the night. "God, you always knew exactly when I'd need you."

The wind shifted again, curling around her, and she let herself imagine Eve there beside her, legs tucked beneath her, cheeks pink from the cold, eyes bright with mischief. She let herself remember the weight of Eve's arm draped across her shoulders during their endless conversations, the sound of her laughter punctuated by half-formed words between fits of giggles.

But now, there was only silence.

Only snow.

Only the letter pressed against her chest so tightly it felt like her own heartbeat.

Maddy closed her eyes and let the grief wash over her. It came in waves, familiar now, rising with the sharp edges of everything she had lost, then softening with the warmth of everything she had once had.

Because some friendships didn't fade. Some loves never left.

And Eve—Eve had never really gone.

She was here.

She was in every memory. In the coffee-stained pages of the old journals they used to scribble in. In the scent of warm vanilla candles that burned on Once Upon A Latte's front counter. In the sound of the boys laughing as they stayed up too late, just like their mother used to.

Eve was here. In this moment. In this new year.

Maddy opened her eyes and sat up straighter, inhaling deeply as the cold air burned her lungs. The ache didn't disappear—it never would—but it shifted, settling into a quieter place inside her.

She folded and smoothed the letter carefully and slipped it back into the envelope before tucking it into her pocket. The paper crackled softly, the sound somehow calming her. Eve had left this for her, had thought of her in those last fragile moments when the weight of leaving must have been unbearable. And if Eve had found the strength to write those words—to reach into the unknown and leave a ghost of herself in the future—then Maddy could find the strength to live them.

The clock inside chimed faintly. She counted the soft notes as they marked the early morning hour.

One. Two. Three.

The first morning of a new year without Eve.

But not without her love.

About The Author
Britt Wolfe

Britt Wolfe was born in Fort McMurray, Alberta, and now lives in Calgary, where she battles snow, writes stories, and cries over Taylor Swift lyrics like the proud elder Swiftie she is. She loves being part of a fan base that's as passionate as it is melodramatic.

She's married to a smoking hot Australian (her words, but also probably everyone else's), and together they parent two fur-babies: Sophie, the most perfect husky in the universe, and Lena, a mischievous cat who keeps them on their toes—and their furniture in shreds.

When Britt's not writing or re-listening to "All Too Well (10 Minute Version)," she's indulging her love for reading, potatoes in all forms, and the colour green. She's also a huge fan of polar bears, tigers, red pandas, otters, Nile crocodiles, and—because they're underrated—donkeys.

Her life is full of love, laughter, and just enough chaos to keep things interesting.

@the.banality.of.britt

BrittWolfe.com

Maddy stood slowly, her legs stiff from the cold. Snow crunched beneath her boots as she turned toward the house. The windows glowed with warmth, the silhouette of Derrick barely visible through the frost-dappled glass.

Before stepping inside, she paused and turned back toward the empty yard. Snow blanketed the ground in a smooth, unbroken sheet, untouched except for the path her footprints had made from the house to the porch swing.

The wind stirred once more, swirling the snow into shimmering spirals across the dark.

Maddy hesitated, heart caught in the space between belief and imagination.

And then, just at the edge of the porch, the snow shifted, moving as though an invisible weight had pressed into it.

A single, distinct footprint. Then another. And another.

Maddy's breath caught in her throat.

There was no sound. No visible explanation. Just the slow, soft imprint of steps that weren't hers.

The footprints stopped beside the swing.

The wind sighed through the branches of the oak tree in the yard.

Maddy squeezed her eyes shut, the tears falling freely down her cheeks as the truth washed over her.

You're still here.

The wind whispered one final time, soft as a memory.

Always.

Maddy pressed her hand to her heart, the weight of Eve's letter solid beneath her palm.

"Happy New Year, Eve," she whispered.

The wind carried her words into the night, swirling the snow into delicate, glowing spirals before letting them fall gently to the ground.

She turned and stepped into the warmth of her home, the door clicking softly behind her.

The snow outside settled into stillness once more, the footprints fading with each passing moment.

But Maddy knew—no matter how deeply time buried those marks in the snow—Eve would always be here.

In the laughter. In the snow. In the space between years.

Holding her hand.

Just like she promised.

You've Reached The End But...
The Stories Never Stop

Songs To Stories is exactly what it sounds like—short, emo[tional,] devastating, romantically charged, and occasionally unhin[ged,] inspired by the one and only Taylor Swift. Because why si[ng a] song when you can spiral into an entire fictional universe[?]

A new novella drops on the 13th and 21st of every month, [so if you have] commitment issues, don't worry—you don't have to wait [long for your] next dose of heartbreak, longing, and characters making [the most] questionable life choices in the name of love.

To keep up with the latest releases, visit BrittWolfe.com [— because you] risk missing out while the rest of us are already crying o[ver the next one.] Your call.

See you at the next emotional wreckage.

Manufactured by Amazon.ca
Bolton, ON

44116767R00042